My Dad is Great

Written by Gaby Goldsack
Illustrated by Sara Walker

PaRragon

Bath New York Singapore Hong Kong Cologne Delhi Melbourne

My dad is **great**.
We have **loads** of fun together.

Designed by Andrea Newton
Language consultant: Betty Root

This is a Parragon book
This edition published by Parragon in 2008

Queen Street House
4 Queen Street
Bath BA1 1HE, UK

ISBN 978-1-84250-574-8
Printed in Malaysia

Today, Mom and Baby are going shopping.
I can't wait to see what adventures Dad
has planned for me while they're away.

My dad is very **Patient.**
He always lets me choose my own clothes.

He doesn't care how long it takes.
I think that, secretly, he really enjoys it!

I wonder if he wants me to
help choose his clothes?

My dad often picks me up from school. He's much, much ... **bigger**

and ... stronger ...
than all the other dads.

And he's a **great** sailor.
He's got a super white sailboat.
It's the fastest boat on ...

the **pond** in the park.

My dad's a **hero.**
He's not afraid of anything.

I hope I'm as **brave** as he is when I grow up!

And he's a great sport. He always lets me win when we play soccer, **but ...**

I pretend not to notice.

Dad and I like the same things.
Hot dogs are our favorite food.

Yummy!

My dad's so **funny**.
He always makes me laugh.

My dad's a **terrific** runner.
He runs around the park much faster
than everyone else.

ZOOOOOM!

And he's a great do-it-yourself man.

Of course, he usually likes me to give him a helping hand. Mom will be really pleased when she sees that we've fixed Baby's crib.

When Dad's around, everything seems fun.
Even ... doing the dishes ...

and ...
sweeping up!

I tell Mom and Baby about the amazing things we've been doing. I can't wait until Baby is old enough to hear all about Dad. Because all dads are special, but ...

my dad is ...

... GR-R-R-EAT!